Grace Dickinson

Songs in the Night

A Collection of Verses

Grace Dickinson

Songs in the Night
A Collection of Verses

ISBN/EAN: 9783337180775

Printed in Europe, USA, Canada, Australia, Japan

Cover: Foto ©Andreas Hilbeck / pixelio.de

More available books at **www.hansebooks.com**

PREFACE.

——o——

A COLLECTION of verses by a poor, bed-ridden
woman in a Union Workhouse, may be fairly
presumed to be too low for the aim of the shafts
of a severe criticism. And the Editor is free to
confess that in his decision to offer them to the
public, he was influenced by the circumstances
under which they were composed.

He was led to this decision by the following
considerations, which he trusts will be accepted
as a sufficient plea for the step he is taking :—

1. They are the *bonâ fide* expression of the
views and feelings of the individual who composed them.

2. They present a striking illustration of
the value of true religion in sustaining the
mind in trial and affliction.

3. Though all that they contain may have been said many times before, yet, emanating as they do from one who was in a condition of poverty and sickness, they seem especially calculated to awaken the interest of those who are in like circumstances.

4. Though taking them on their intrinsic merits, they may not present sufficient claims for publication, the Editor hopes they are not so deficient in worth, but that, with the above considerations in the scale, their appearance before the world may be justified.

That He who chooses " the weak things of the world to confound the things which are mighty," may grant His abundant blessing upon everything in this unpretending little book that is in accordance with His revealed truth, is the sincere prayer of

THE EDITOR.

Halifax, April 8th, 1863.

CONTENTS.

—o—

		Page.
	ACCOUNT OF THE AUTHOR	9
I.	PRAISE AND THANKSGIVING	19
II.	INCARNATION, SUFFERINGS, &c., OF CHRIST	26
III.	CONFESSION OF SIN, AND SUPPLICATION FOR MERCY	31
IV.	BLESSEDNESS OF THE RELIGION OF CHRIST	38
V.	PRAYER	52
VI.	AFFLICTION	55
VII.	PERSONAL RECOLLECTIONS	59
VIII.	EXPRESSIVE OF THE AUTHOR'S OWN FEELINGS	65
IX.	TO THE CHAIRMAN OF THE BOARD OF GUARDIANS	76
X.	ON THE DEATHS OF INMATES OF THE WORKHOUSE	78
XI.	FOR THE YOUNG	81
XII.	MISCELLANEOUS	83

BRIEF ACCOUNT OF THE AUTHOR.

BY THE EDITOR.

Grace Dickinson became an inmate of the Halifax Union Workhouse on the 1st of February, 1861. She had at that time a very juvenile appearance for her years, and seemed in an advanced stage of consumption. I regarded her as a person whose days on earth were fast hastening to a close, and addressed her from time to time on the simple elementary truths of the Gospel of Christ. She was always glad to see me, and received my remarks with interest, but she spoke very little, and her weakness appeared to be such as to render it undesirable for her to speak more than was needed. Hence it was some time before I had any adequate idea of her intelligence or piety. In one of her pieces addressed to me, not adopted in this collection, she thus describes her feelings on the occasion of those first visits :—

> "I did welcome you at first
> _I did list with eagerness,
> When you spoke of Jesus Christ,
> And His willingness to bless.
>
> When at first you spoke to me,
> I did long to talk with you,
> But my timid heart did beat,
> And my weakness came anew."

It was not until the May following that I received any intimation of the capabilities of G. Dickinson in the line which has gained for her a humble distinction. In that month an aged woman occupying the next bed to hers, who had been about five years in the house, and had spent the greater part of that time in this one room, was taken away by death. She had gained the respect of the other inmates by the maintenance of a consistently pious course of conduct, and her departure from the lowly circle was felt as a bereavement. On the Saturday of that week, G. D. said to me, " I have been trying, Sir, to improve Rachel Dawson's death, by composing some verses, and I shall feel obliged if you will be kind enough to take them down some time." I was agreeably surprised by the statement, and at once prepared to comply with her request. She gave the first of the four verses which appear on page 78 :—

" Poor Rachel is gone,—what a happy release, &c."

At the close of the first verse her strength and memory seemed to fail, and the remaining verses were dictated on my next call. The piece was inserted in each of the Halifax papers for the following Saturday, May 18th, and among the little articles of property found under her pillow after her death was the newspaper containing these verses. The Monday following she dictated the verses, " On Affliction," at page 55 :—

" 'Tis Thee, great God, 'tis Thee we love, &c."

She had composed these previously to the verses on Rachel Dawson, but does not seem to have had the courage to introduce them, until emboldened by the favourable reception of the others. She assured me, in reply to my inquiry, that the language here employed was the real expression of her own heartfelt experience.

The ice being now fairly broken, and the approach of summer bringing with it a slight accession of strength to her debilitated frame, a week scarcely ever passed, but she had one or more pieces ready for me whenever I found it convenient to take them down. After a while she herself wrote her verses on a slate, and I copied them. Her handwriting was fair, and her orthography tolerable.

But in the last months of her life, her verses were supplied to me in a manner which was at once novel and interesting. Sarah Thomas, a deaf and dumb girl of about sixteen, who had learnt to read and write at the Doncaster School for the Deaf and Dumb, became an inmate of the Workhouse in consequence of fits. G. DICKINSON learnt the Deaf and Dumb Alphabet, and was soon able to engage in conversation by the fingers with her mute companion. And as the little strength that she had became more and more impaired, and she was incapacitated for the exercise of writing, she dictated her verses letter by letter to the deaf and dumb girl, who wrote them on the slate at intervals, as the composer's feebleness permitted. When I saw the two persons

thus employed, I thought the scene one of the most interesting I had ever looked upon ; and I would take occasion to
suggest that if the book which is now presented to the
world contains nothing new in its subject matter, there is
certainly something new in the manner of its production.

It may be inferred from the language used in many parts
of this collection, that the author had experienced her full
share of trial and affliction in this world. It was even so.
Her husband for several years manifested an aberration of
mind, which proved to her a source of inexpressible trouble,
and the cup of her sorrow was at length filled to overflow-
ing by the melancholy fact of his laying violent hands upon
himself. After his death she went in an enfeebled state of
health to work at a factory, and her exertions for the
support of herself and her children resulted in the entire
breaking up of her constitution. After eighteen months
of widowhood, spent in deep poverty and affliction, she
was brought to the Workhouse at the age of thirty-five,
in a state of utter prostration.

It has been stated that she rallied a little as the season
advanced. She was able to sit up during a part of each
day and to attend Divine Service on the Sabbath. When
the cold weather came she was again confined to her bed,
and it appeared exceedingly improbable that she would
survive through the winter of 1861-2. But her days were
prolonged, and with the return of spring, signs of improvement were again visible. She took her seat in the summer
with the less enfeebled occupants of the sick room, though
not so frequently as in the corresponding season of the
previous year. At the close of July she had a severe attack
which it was thought would prove the messenger of death,
and although she survived it, the remaining six months of
her life were passed in a state of extreme debility.

Such was the condition of our author—such were her
circumstances at the time when she composed her verses.
Nevertheless, it always appeared to me that the mental
exercise involved in their production did not impose a
burden, but afforded a relief, as she herself frequently inti-
mates in her lines. Had I thought otherwise, I should not
have encouraged her in the task by taking them down.
Many of them are literally " songs in the night," having
been composed in the silent hours of darkness, or when that
silence was disturbed by the moans of the suffering, the

restlessness of the aged and superannuated, or the hard
and audible breathing of the dying; and all of them have
been produced in the *night of affliction.* Hence I could
not think of a more appropriate title.

That the expressions of adoration, trust in God, resignation to His will, delight in His mercy, and devotedness to
His glory, are the *bona fide* language of the heart of her
who employed them, no one who had any acquaintance
with her would for a moment doubt. She exemplified in
her life the principles which furnished the subjects of her
lines. Though frequently called to "walk through the
valley of the shadow of death," it was ever manifest that
she "feared no evil, for the rod and the staff" of the
Almighty " comforted her;" and I am persuaded that her
habitual peace and serenity of mind was one principal
means of the lengthening out of her days to a later period
than her extreme feebleness would have led any one to
anticipate. And I believe that all the inmates of the sick
rooms were impressed, more or less deeply, with a sense of
the value of true religion, as exemplified in the spirit and
conduct of GRACE DICKINSON. During the whole of her
long affliction, I never heard of her mourning or repining,
and although with respect to general intelligence she was
greatly in advance of those about her, she never assumed
any importance on such grounds. Her general influence,
in the "long sick room" where she was lodged, had a
visibly beneficial tendency, and a more kindly tone of
feeling was the result of her presence. She was of great
service to the more thoughtful and serious of the sick inmates, and she embraced every opportunity of christian
usefulness that lay within her reach. When there were a
number in the room able to read and willing to engage in
the exercise, and she was sufficiently well to join them,
she induced them to assemble in the evenings at a convenient hour to read the scriptures together. And I have
reason to believe that her object in learning to talk by the
fingers with the deaf and dumb girl, was to interest, instruct, and benefit her, and that the employment of her as
amanuensis was an afterthought.

One test of the sincerity of our professions of thankful-
ness to the bounteous Giver of all good, is the grateful
acknowledgment of our obligations to those who are the
means by which that good is communicated. By this test
the professions of GRACE DICKINSON would well bear to be

tried. She was uniformly respectful in her demeanour towards all the officers, and grateful for whatever was done for her. The saying that " paupers are unthankful " has passed into a proverb, but in this case we can point to a most signal exception.

In the winter of 1862-3, the symptoms of approaching dissolution appeared unmistakeable. But the prospect of her departure was contemplated with perfect serenity. She felt that she was in the hands of her gracious Saviour and Redeemer, and she exercised an unwavering trust in His wisdom and love. She was invariably " patient in tribulation," and although sometimes depressed in her extreme feebleness, and "in heaviness through manifold temptations," she was never led into any distressing doubts as to her eternal safety. Until the last week of her life she did not seem to think that her departure was so near as the medical attendant and those about her apprehended it would be, her long continued sickness and frequent rallying after prostration doubtless causing her to regard this attack as resembling her former ones. She certainly was not influenced either by the fear of death or any undue " love of life," for her recognition of God's hand in all things that concerned her, and her resignation to His will, were habitual.

On the morning of Thursday, January 22, I was sent for to see her, the messenger stating that she was thought to be dying. She revived a little during the day, and expressed, in the last extremity, the same "good hope through grace" which had sustained her in so much trial and affliction, and had so often inspired her humble lines. Next morning she was less exhausted than on the preceding day, but was still exceedingly feeble, and she requested me to pray that she might be released. During the day I repeated to her the verses " On Affliction " which appear at page 55. This seemed to afford her pleasure, and although it was evident that she could not long survive, the apparent improvement in her condition was such as to avert all apprehension on my part that this was the last time I should speak to her. During that night she was so far revived as to be able to raise herself on each attack of coughing, and she conversed cheerfully with the persons who sat up with her. This proved the brief respite from exhaustion, which after lingering sickness is so often the immediate precursor of the final change. At about six o'clock on Saturday morning she was engaged in offering up what the attendant called a " very beautiful prayer," and while in this exercise the stroke of death came upon her. She continued about four hours in a state of unconsciousness, when her spirit passed away to the presence of her Redeemer, so quietly that the precise moment could not be ascertained. I entered the room just in time to witness the closing scene, and the occasion was one that I shall not soon forget. There is perhaps no one room in the entire parish of Halifax, (except the corresponding one on the men's side of the house,) where the occurrence of death is so frequent as the room in which she died. It is very large, and filled with beds occupied by the sick alone, many of whom are brought to the Union in the last stages of disease. But common as death is to the inmates of that room, the death of GRACE DICKINSON was felt by every one of them to be an event of no common character. All seemed impressed with the thought that they were losing one whose Christian life and deportment had addressed itself to their consciences. Every sound was hushed, and many were in tears. And when all was over, and the writer prayed that the event might be sanctified to all who were present, and exhorted them to prepare for the time when their own summons should come, and to follow her who had departed as she had followed Christ, he felt in addition to the lessons he had learnt from her in her lifetime, this truth impressed upon his mind with unwonted power, that the distinctions in human society, needful as they are in themselves, and right and scriptural in their place, are after all, of comparatively trivial character. Whether in the palace or the cottage, or even within the walls of the Union Workhouse, " Precious in the sight of the Lord is the death of His saints." And while fully assured that this poor and deeply afflicted woman has passed away to that blessed land where sorrow and sighing are fled away, where pain is never felt, and where poverty never enters, where every face is radiant with joy, where every head wears a crown, and every hand carries a palm, my hope and prayer for myself and the readers of this brief and imperfect sketch is, that our last end may be like hers.

Poor Grace Dickinson was ever ready to acknowledge that the heavy trials with which she was visited arose in a great degree from a want of prudence and a departure from Christian consistency, with respect to the most important step in life which a young person can take. The very night before she died, she said, in allusion to this, that she hoped her case would prove a warning to other young women. And thankful should I be if any such, on reading this brief sketch and reflecting that the subject of it might, but for one untoward step, have filled and adorned a comparatively respectable position in society, and have lived to a good old age, instead of passing her best days in privation and untold sorrow, and being cut off with pining sickness when the noon of life was scarcely reached, and ending her days in the Union Workhouse—thankful, I say, should I be if any, on thus reflecting, be induced to "ask counsel of the Lord" before they enter upon one of the most momentous of all engagements, and to cease from following their inclinations when those inclinations do not accord with the path of duty.

The question will naturally be asked to what extent the following collection in its present form has been indebted to the editorial pen. This question I would anticipate by a full and candid statement. I am responsible for the selection, the arrangement, the orthography, and the greater number of the headings. The emendations in the text are by no means numerous and are of verbal character. What may be looked upon as the best passages owe nothing to my pen. I have not attempted to beautify or adorn even by a touch, but have confined myself to the correction of the most obvious inaccuracies. I have endeavoured to repair any *broken joint*, and have given my best assistance to a *limping line*, but this is all that I have done. In two instances where the required correction involved an alteration in the structure of the language, the fact is signified by a note.

Had the whole of the verses been printed which she composed during the two years of her Workhouse life, the book would have numbered more than one hundred and forty pages. But as her critical acumen was not equal to her capability of verse making, her compositions greatly varied in merit, some of them being inferior to those which are selected. The same piece also would sometimes present considerable variation in different parts. When this was the case I threw out the more faulty, and adopted the better portion, and this will account for the fragmentary character of some of the pieces. It may be thought by the more literary readers, that the collection would well have borne a closer pruning ; but I would repeat the plea which

I have urged in the Preface, and would further add that if any publication ever possessed a fair claim upon the indulgence of the critical reader, such claim is surely presented by the present one. Some pieces of rather commonplace character have been admitted, on the ground that they afforded light on the past history of the author, and others, because they seemed to present a photographic representation, as it were, of her mental idiosyncracy.

She herself accomplished a little in the way of revision. I was accustomed to mention to her any marked inaccuracy and leave her to correct it. In some instances she happily succeeded, but at other times she could not correct the sense without sacrificing the rhyme or metre. The chief errors consisted in the misapplication of such words as do not commonly occur in the conversation of uneducated persons. Less frequently, there were faults in the logical construction of her sentences, though the meaning intended was always evident. The common rules of syntax were rarely broken, and still more rarely was any alteration required in the rhyme or rhythm. Some of the few deviations from the strict rhyme which occur in the collection, are occasioned by my having had to change a word in order to express correctly the meaning of the author.

The educational advantages possessed by GRACE DICKINSON were perhaps not greater than those which ordinarily fall to the lot of the factory operatives of this district, except that when in her teens she learnt the elements of grammar. She was from a child very much given to reading. But her opportunities of acquiring literary and general information must have been very limited, and she never mixed with cultivated society. Her verses seem (unconsciously perhaps) framed on the model of the devotional hymn books to which she has had access, but I do not believe that she has knowingly borrowed a line from any quarter. It will be seen from the collection that her subjects embrace but a narrow range. I occasionally suggested a variation of topics, (as for instance, scripture characters and narratives,) which she would have been glad to pursue had her strength been a little recruited. It was not a task but a relief to her to give expression in verse to the thoughts which flowed in their accustomed channel; but to strike out a new path, even within the limits of her comparatively small range of information, would have implied an effort for which her mind, sympathizing with an exhausted frame, was altogether unfitted.

Whether GRACE DICKINSON really possessed the gift of poetry is a question which I would rather leave to the decision of impartial and considerate judges. I have nowhere ventured to dignify her verses by the name of poetry ; but, unless I mistake, I have seen that word applied to compositions possessing as little claim to the epithet as those which are now submitted to public notice ; and my own opinion is, that without some endowment in that direction, she could never, with the disadvantages under which she laboured, have produced lines of so passable a character.

But whatever may be said as to the spirit of *poetry*, I have no hesitancy in speaking to the spirit of *piety* which breathes through these humble effusions. I can say that they are truly scriptural and spiritual, and I would hope that their simple and unpretending character will prove a recommendation to the class for which I deem them best calculated to be useful.

GRACE DICKINSON lost three children in infancy, and three have survived her. The eldest, a boy, resides with her friends, and is employed at a factory. The two youngest accompanied her to the Workhouse, where they still remain. Before her departure she obtained a promise from me that I would take a friendly interest in their welfare. The boy is ten, and the girl five years of age.

It is intended to place in the Savings' Bank whatever amount may be realized by the sale of this little book, to allow the interest to accumulate, and to expend the amount for their benefit when they leave the Workhouse, or place it at their disposal in after life. The Guardians have generously contributed a portion of the expense of printing, and it is hoped that other kind friends will assist in defraying the remainder, so that not simply the *profits* but the entire *proceeds* may be devoted to the object contemplated. And all who purchase and promote the sale of the book, will have the satisfaction of knowing that in so doing they are contributing to the assistance of the orphan children of one who was of the "household of faith," and whose only legacy was a mother's prayers.*

THOMAS SNOW.

RHODES STREET, HALIFAX.

* See p. 74.

SONGS IN THE NIGHT.

———o———

I.

Praise and Thanksgiving.

I.

GREAT Builder of this universal frame!
From Thee all Nature's beauteous order came.
All wisdom and perfection spring from Thee,
And fill the earth and the great teeming sea.
Surpassing wonders, wonderful art Thou,
Maker of summer's sun and winter's snow.
Great in Thy power, and in Thy nature pure,
Unchangeably the same Thou shalt endure.
How holy, wise, and righteous are Thy laws,
Which man hath dar'd to break and to oppose!
But O, Thou just One, Thou wilt punish sin!
And we may fear, for guilty we have been.
But, Lord, there is a volume Thou hast sent,
That calls upon all sinners to repent.
It tells us Jesus suffered all our due,
No matter what our nation, or our hue.
  Giver of all the good that we possess,
Permit Thy creature man Thy name to bless
For all Thy goodness,—but the most of all
For Jesus, our Redeemer from the Fall.

II.

BLEST Providence,*—my glory, and my stay,
My firm support, my comfort here on earth;
What though my path be dark, the thought
     " Thou art"
Is precious to my trembling, hoping soul.
But for the thoughts of Thee I could not live;
I could not bear the sorrows that I meet,
The daily, hourly sorrows that start up,
And haunt my spirit like a frightful dream,
And crowd my path, perplexing human skill.
All praise, all adoration be to Thee,
That in the midst of this terrestrial scene,
Sweet hope doth rise, and hover round my soul,
And whispers peace to my tumultuous breast;
She points to Thee, good Providence,* to Thee,
Giver of immortality to man.
O, stamp Thine image on this fallen soul,
And seal divine impressions on this breast!
Yea, such as cares will not make me forget,
Nor time will e'er efface, nor death destroy.

III.

GREAT Father of the human race,
    Thy bounty feeds the poor;
'Tis from the treasures of thy grace
    We draw our daily store.

---

  * A slight misapprehension of the meaning of the word
" Providence" is betrayed here, but the Editor has not
thought it necessary to interfere with the flow of the lines,
as the meaning intended is sufficiently plain.

The earthly comforts that we prize
From Thy kind hand proceed,
And daily as fresh blessings rise
The pleasing fact we read.

But O, for greater things than these,
Things that more nobly shine,
Thy name we would adore and bless,
And utter praise divine!

IV.

THE last of God's promises cannot be had,
To-day and for ever with freshness they're clad.
They shine forth in darkness, their lustre is bright,
They beam on the spirit 'midst sin and its blight.

The last of God's mercies can never be known,
So great is their number, so widely they're strown.
His bounty provideth for man and for beast:
He careth for all, the greatest and least.

V.

THY ways become Thyself, O God,
In wisdom so immense;
But they are little understood.
By reason, or by sense.

Thy ways, to our short sighted views,
Are all past finding out;
They puzzle the profoundest views,
They puzzle human thought.

But the announcements of Thy love
  Are pleasant and are good ;
Refreshing to our souls they prove,
  Through Jesu's precious blood.

Thy justice all our fears doth move,
  Thy wisdom we admire,
But the sweet tokens of thy love
  Our confidence inspire.

Only through Jesus can we hope
  For comfort and for peace ;
To Him alone can faith look up,
  And triumph in His grace.

VI.

Fountain of goodness, Source of grace,
Author of order, light and love,
Accept our poor but humble praise,
For all Thy goodness which we prove.

We bless Thee for the Saviour dear,
Through Him alone our comforts rise,
All the enjoyments we have here,
Or hope to share beyond the skies.

We bless Thee for Thy holy Book,
Blest revelation to our race !
When we within its pages look,
Grant us the teachings of Thy grace.

We bless Thee for the Sabbath Day,
That holy, that appointed rest;
It gladdens us while here we stay;
Of all the days, this is the best.

We bless Thee for thy Spirit's light,
Afforded through a Saviour's blood.
Lord, ever teach us what is right,
And lead us to eternal good!

VII.

WHAT mercies are our daily lot,
Mercies that we do not deserve!
What mercies that we have forgot!
What mercies still are in reserve!

Life is a mercy truly great,
The avenue of all that's dear;
None justly can appreciate
Its worth, or its enjoyments here.

Our life might be one wretched scene;
Despair might each enjoyment kill;
But smiling hope steps in between,
And makes all good feel better still.

Mercy attends us all our way,
And fences us around with care;
Mercy provides the light of day;
There's mercy in the very air.

Lord, Thou art merciful indeed,
Thy works declare this cheering fact;
But in Thy holy word we read
Mercy is Thy delightful act.

VIII.

BLEST be the Lord for kindness shown,
Here comforts in my path are strown,
    And cluster in my way;
Whichever way I turn mine eyes,
Comforts and mercies round me rise,
    Cheering my workhouse stay.

Blest be the Lord for every good,
For life, for raiment, and for food,
    For comfort, and for peace,
For shelter from the wintry blast,
For safety till its storms be past,
    And all its roughness cease.

Blest be the Lord who brought me here,
Mercies in this event appear,
    Unlook'd for, and unsought;
Nor the less sweet and welcome they,
Surprising me each passing day;
    In season they are brought.

Blest be the Lord, yea, blessed still,
In ease or pain, in good or ill,
    In life or death the same;
It is the Lord who does me good,
Gives me all things through Jesu's blood,
    Through Him accepts my claim.

Blest be the Lord for gifts divine,
In holy intercourse they shine,
   And thus augment our love ;
In fellowship with Him and His,
What foretastes of the promis'd bliss,
   Foretastes of heaven above !

IX.

Yes, I bless Thee, heavenly Father,
   Though the cross on earth is given,
Tribulations here may gather,
   Fondest ties on earth be riven,
     Yet I bless Thee
   That there is a promis'd heaven.

This consoles and this uplifts me ;
   How transporting is the thought !
Though the tempter here may sift me,
   There his siftings are forgot :
     Jesus, lead me
   Where temptation dwelleth not.

Lord, I love Thee, and Thou knowest
   How I long to see Thy face ;
Though I am the very lowest,
   All unworthy of Thy grace.
     Yet, O give me
   In that heavenly land a place !

II.

The Incarnation, Sufferings, &c. of Christ.

I.

CHRISTMAS.

LET music break on this blest morn,
And sweetly echo back to heaven,
For lo ! the promised Son is born,
The long expected One is given.

Of old the prophets wrote of Him,
Predicting this most glad event,
And we, in one united hymn,
Now celebrate the Saviour sent.

In heaven the angels sing of Him,
And wonder at His mighty love;
On earth we gladly chant the theme.
Thus joining in the song above.

Thus angels, prophets, sinners sing,
With all the numbers sav'd in heaven,
And hail Thy advent, Saviour, King :
One glorious strain to all is given.

Nor can we sing a worthier name,
Or sing of love so great as Thine ;
No ! endless honours Thou dost claim ;
Thy name and love are both divine.

II.

Jesus spake as never man did speak before ;
Jesus preach'd the blessed gospel to the poor ;
Jesus brought a better, sweeter land to view ;
Jesus did our everlasting good pursue ;
Jesus came in poverty for us to live ;
Jesus has enduring riches now to give ;
Jesus had a crown of thorns put on His head ;
Jesus now wears a crown of glory in its stead ;
Jesus bore our heavy load of sin and guilt ;
Jesus sweat blood when our sad punishment He felt ;
Jesus was a man of sorrow and of grief ;
Jesus can succour us, and send relief ;
Jesus lov'd, but not as selfish mortals love ;
His love's great depths 'twill take eternity to prove.

III.

Sing, every land, of Jesu's love.
Who left his shining throne above,
And pitied man who trod the path
That leads to everlasting death.

He came to seek that which was lost,
By every wind of doctrine tost ;
He came to teach His doctrine pure.
And seal the Father's mercies sure.

He came to die for guilty man,
And finish all salvation's plan,
To die that we might dwell above,
And ever sing redeeming love.

IV.

Jesus, we bless Thee for Thy *love*,
  Unmerited and free,
'Tis higher than the heaven above,
  And deeper than the sea!

Jesus, we bless Thee for thy *truth*,
  So plain and yet so grand,
'Tis all sufficient in our youth,
  And when with age we bend.

Jesus, we bless Thee for Thy *grace*,
  So cheering and so sweet,
Still give our trembling souls a place
  Near Thy lov'd mercy seat.

Jesus, we bless Thee for Thy *care*,
  A tender Shepherd Thou,
Who kindly listens to each prayer,
  Who kindly helps us through.

Jesus, we bless Thee for the *way*
  That leads to heaven on high;
We bless Thee that we cannot stay
  Where tears bedim the eye.

Jesus, we bless Thee for the *hope*
  Of better days to come;
O may Thy grace still bear us up,
  Till we arrive at home!

Jesus, we bless Thee for Thy *life*,
  So holy and so good;

O help us evermore to strive
 To imitate our God !

Jesus, we bless Thee for Thy *death*
 Upon the accursed tree ;
O grant to us a stronger faith,
 May we more trustful be.

V.

CHRIST'S RESURRECTION AND INTERCESSION.

WHY do we fear death's icy touch ?
Or tremble at the grave so much ?
Jesus hath sanctified the tomb,
And left therein a sweet perfume.

Long in the grave He did not lay,*
But rose again on the third day,
To live for ever, evermore :
Let all on earth His name adore.

How highly favour'd those He met,
While forty days He tarried yet !
His salutations, O how full !
Peace, peace to each believing soul.

Hence is our hope (because he rose,
And conquer'd all that could oppose)
That He will bring us conquerors through,
And give us palms of victory too.

* Lie.

He hath ascended up on high,
To plead our cause above the sky;
He listens to, presents each prayer,
And adds His intercession there.

How full of tenderness He pleads,
He tells the Father all our needs,
Gently reminds Him of the grief
That He endured for our relief.

'Tis through His merits and His blood,
That we approach unto our God:
No other name our souls can save,
Nor quell the terrors of the grave.

III.

Confession of Sin, & Supplication for Mercy.

I.

FORGIVE our carelessness, O Lord,
　And all our wicked ways;
We think too little of Thy word,
　So full of promis'd grace.

Our understandings, O how dark!
　How blinded through our sin!
By nature not the smallest spark
　Of light can break within.

By nature, Lord, we love not Thee,
　Nor any of Thy ways,
But through Thy Spirit, grant that we
　May holiness embrace.

Our hearts are hard, we need Thy love,
　To soften and to draw;
Nought but Thy grace sin's ice can move,
　And make a lasting thaw.

By nature we are dead in sin:
　Our dying souls awake!
Implant new principles within,
　For our Redeemer's sake.

O, may Thy Spirit's piercing rays
　Our darken'd souls illume!
O, may the sunshine of Thy grace
　Disperse our nature's gloom!

II.

O, I could weep ten thousand tears,
When I look back on my past years !
Beeause I've sinn'd against the Lord,
And did not heed His sacred word.

Lord, turn this heart so wicked, vile,
From all iniquity and guile,
And give me grace to follow Thee,
Till here my days shall number'd be.

III.

A GUILTY sinner I have been,
     A rebel to the Lord ;
Oppress'd with fears, and guilt, and sin,
     I cling unto His word.

With throbbing heart, and earnest thought,
     Its statements I have read ;
Jesus a full salvation brought,
     When on the cross He bled.

O may my life be hid with Thee,
     Faithful, unchanging Friend,
Grant persevering grace to mc,
     And help me to the end.

Then will I bless Thy name in death,
     And triumph in Thy love,
Jesus, sweet Finisher of faith,
     In the full sight above !

IV.

Jesus, how long shall I remain
  So lukewarm and so cold,
At ease in sin's enchanting plain,
  And yielding to its hold ?

I own my heart is full of sin,
  To evil it is bent;
I own its wickedness within,
  I own it and lament.

I mourn my distance from Thy love,
  My distance from all good,
Give me Thy Spirit from above,
  And lead me unto God !

V.

Spirit of all consolation,
  Come and chase away my fears;
O, how sad my situation,
  Till Thy grace to me appears !

I profess to be believing,
  Yet my faithlessness is great;
But, the Holy Ghost receiving,
  Soon my faith will animate.*

I profess that I am loving,
  Yet how full of coldness still !
But the Spirit in me moving,
  With His grace can quickly fill.

* Used as a neuter verb.

B

I profess to be repenting,
   Yet how careless every day,
Till the Spirit, truth presenting,
   Shows the error of my way.

I profess that I am living
   To the Lord,—and yet I fail,
Till to me the Spirit giving,
   In His strength I then prevail.

I profess that I am seeking
   A bright kingdom in the skies ;
But on earth my soul is fixing,
   Till the Spirit bids me rise.

I profess to be a stranger,
   And my foes surround this place ;
Yet I oft forget my danger,
   Till again arous'd by grace.

What availeth my profession,
   If my heart belies the same ?
Lord, give me a true possession,
   Grace to glorify Thy name !

VI.

I FEEL unworthy, Lord, indeed,
   Unworthy of thy care ;
Yet on Thy bounties I do feed,
   And every comfort share.

I feel unworthy, Lord, of all
   The blessings Thou dost give;

Unworthy on Thy name to call,
  Or 'neath Thy smile to live.

Unworthy of Thy children's bread,
  Their prospects, or their rest;
Yet with their manna I am fed,
  And of their good possess'd.

Unworthy of their thought or care,
  Less than the least I fall;
Yet still their kindness I do share,
  O Lord, reward them all!

VII.

JESUS, a poor sinner save!
Pardon for my sins I crave:
Perishing, and weak, and lost;
With temptation rudely tost.

Jesus, to Thy cross I flee:
I must perish without Thee.
O, assure me of Thy love!
Register my name above.

Give to me a contrite heart;
Bid all pride from me depart:
Let no idol dwell within,
Save me from the love of sin.

Be my strength, and be my light;
O, be with me day and night;
Be my everlasting Friend;
With Thy truth and love defend,

Thou dost my condition see,
I have nought to bring to Thee,
Nought but this bad heart of mine;
And no arm can save but Thine.

Thou didst die for the unjust;
Thou art therefore all my trust.
I would Thy disciple be;
Jesus, O accept of me!

Give me riches not of earth,
Riches of eternal worth,
An inheritance divine,
Where Thy holy ones do shine.

VIII.

Can I, a sinner living,
    A living one complain?
Forgetting sin is giving
    Life's bitterness and pain?

Can I be found indulging
    A sinful state of mind,
Without the truth divulging,
    That sin leaves woe behind?

Can I be found complaining
    Of all and every thing?
Such discontent prevailing,
    Its punishment will bring.

Can I be found abusing
    The life already given,
Without all good refusing
    That comes direct from heaven?

Can I be found insulting
  The Giver of all grace,
In wickedness exulting?
  Such conduct, O how base!

Can I be found denying
  My blessed Saviour here?
His holy cross defying?
  Perdition then is near.

Can I be undecided
  In my Redeemer's cause?
And have my heart divided?
  Then I His work oppose.

Can I go on in sinning,
  Without a sigh or tear?
Then Satan ground is winning,
  And I have cause to fear.

Can I be onward pressing
  To yonder mansions fair,
My Master's mind possessing,
  And wish not all to share?

Can I feel sin's sad deluge,
  And yet delay to flee
To Christ the only Refuge?
  Woe then is unto me.

Can I, O blessed Saviour,
  Share daily in Thy grace,
Unworthy such a favour,
  And yet withhold Thy praise?

IV.

The Blessedness of the Religion of Christ.

I.

CHILD of God, tell sinners round
Whence most comforts you have found.
In religion there is bliss,
Ev'n in such a place as this.*

It is pleasant, it is sweet,
'Tis with happiness complete,
It affords unshaken peace,
And its comforts still increase.

Tell it in the Sabbath School:
O, explain Redemption's rule!
Without faith, condemned we lie:
With it, condemnations fly.

Pastors, faithful still abide,
Preach our Jesus crucified:
Preach the wonders of the cross,
Ours the gain, but His the loss!

Strive to win the rising race,
Through the Spirit of His grace:
Strive to win them to His love.
O, may all its sweetness prove!

Tell the great, the worthy deed,
How the Son of God did bleed,

* The Workhouse.

That we might be all forgiv'n,
That we might have peace with heav'n.

Tell it in the stately halls,
And within the prison walls,
Tell it in the humble cot,
Never let it be forgot.

Tell it in the workhouse too ;
'Tis as sweet refreshing dew ;
'Twill bring comfort to the heart,
When all comforts else depart.

It is worthy to be told,
Worthy to be writ in gold,
Worthy to be hail'd by all,
Who are ruin'd by the Fall.

Send it o'er the ocean wide,
To each clime where men reside ;
To each colour, tongue, and age,
Send the ever blessed page !

Tell them of the Son of man,
How His course on earth He ran ;
How He died His love to prove,
How He loves beyond all love !

Christians, O, in heart be one,
Seeking glory not your own :
For immortal spirits care ;
Spread His word in praise and prayer.

II.

'Tis Jesus we seek, the Pearl of great price!
Though helpless and weak, He pities our cries.
In Him there are hid rich treasures of grace,
Though others forbid, we'll seek His blest face.

The wicked may laugh, the worldly may sneer,
But pleasures are ours when Jesus is near;
In Him we confide, through Him come to God,
No other beside can do our souls good.

'Tis Jesus we seek, for Jesus we need;
Though sinful and weak, for us He doth plead.
His love, it is great, and sovereign, and free,
His name ever must our refuge still be.

Our troubles through sin are many and great;
Without and within, it saddens our state;
But He bids us come, His word is most true;
Poor sinners, there's room for me and for you.

III.

Jesus liv'd and died to save me,
    Prompted by eternal love;
His eternal self he gave me;
    What could more His kindness prove?

Now to save me He is able,
    For this very end He died;
This is not a cunning fable,
    'Tis a truth that must abide.

'Tis in vain that Satan rushes,
  Like an armed man, on me;
Tenderness and pity gushes,
  Blessed Jesus, still from Thee.

'Tis in vain that he accuses,
  Brings ten thousand sins to view;
Jesus never one refuses,
  Who doth His forgiveness sue.

Yes, I know my sins are many,
  Deeply I bewail the same;
But salvation is for any
  Who believe in Jesu's name.

'Tis as free as can be given,
  'Tis as free as free can be,
As the very air of heaven,
  As the water in the sea!

'Tis as great as can be needed,
  As complete as can be made:
Sinners, pass it not unheeded,
  Seek therein to be array'd.

IV.

SEEK we good unmix'd with ill,
Good each aching void to fill,
Good substantial?—'tis not here,
Earth is not its native sphere.

Seek we happiness to share,
Undisturb'd with woe and care?
Vain we seek on every hand,
Earth is not its native land.

Seek we pleasure free from pain,
Unpolluted with a stain?
Seek it here?—then we are wrong:
It does not to earth belong.

Seek ye friends and friendships true,
That will bring no pain to you?
Seek them here?   Ah, sad mistake!
Sin made them the earth forsake.

Why seek fruit on barren trees?
Why seek health amidst disease?
Or for peace 'midst seats of war?
Or for rest where tumults are?

Mortals tossed up and down,
See your schemes like bubbles blown:
Thus 'twill be, if earth you trust,
Moth will eat, and damp will rust.

How infatuated they
Who are bent on their own way!
Disappointment must be theirs,
Sorrow, trouble, vexing cares.

Do you wish for good secure?
Good that ever must endure?
Seek it in its proper place,
Seek it in redeeming grace.

Sinner, turn thy thoughts on high,
Far above this changing sky;
Seek for good in God alone,
Who doth hear when call'd upon.

He hath sent His word to tell,
That He loves poor sinners well;
So you need not be afraid,
But, through Jesus, seek His aid.

He can make the wretched blest:
Of all friends He is the best:
He will make you rich indeed,
Granting help in time of need.

Good through Jesus now secure,
For no other good is sure.
Seek, through Jesus' dying love,
Seek a home in heaven above.

v.

SWEET is the spring time of the year,
When the bright cuckoo sings her lay.
How pleasant 'tis her voice to hear,
As still we travel on our way!

Sweet is the summer's evening breeze,
When all around is still and calm,
And gently wave the aged trees
Around the cottage and the farm.

Sweet is the time of merry youth,
When hearts are light, and cares unknown,

Before we feel the mournful truth,
That life with bitter seeds is sown.

Sweet is the time of precious health,
When we are active, well, and strong,
Sweeter than many stores of wealth :
How sweet these moments pass along !

Sweet is the intercourse of friends,
When heart to heart in union meet,
When fellowship with friendship blends ;
O, then how pleasant, and how sweet !

Sweet is the memory of the dead ;
How oft to us their names are dear,
Although their spirits hence are fled,
No more to mingle with us here !

Sweet is the holy book of truth,
'Tis worth perusing with great care ;
If we but heeded it in youth,
We should be sav'd from many a snare.

Sweet is the Sabbath of the Lord,
When we can meet his people dear,
And listen to His holy word,
And learn His name to love and fear.

Sweet are the moments spent in prayer,
And pleading with our gracious God ;
This soothes our mind when fill'd with care,
When we approach through Jesus' blood.

Talk we of sweetness here below
'Midst imperfection, change, and sin,
In heaven its fulness we shall know,
When Jesus bids us enter in.

VI.

WEARIED with scenes of earth,
　　Jesus, to Thee I cry ;
Wearied with sin's debasing mirth.
　　I raise my thoughts on high :

Far better sights to see,
　　Far sweeter sounds to hear,
O that the power were given to me
　　To leave this guilty sphere !

Jesus, I bless Thy name,
　　I bless Thy sovereign love,
Which stands unchangeably the same,
　 - As every day I prove.

My comforts spring from Thee,
　　Whether of earth or heaven ;
And every good that comes to me,
　　By Thy kind hand is given.

VII.

CHRISTIAN, time is passing by,
Thy redemption draweth nigh,
Time momentous, fraught with grace,
Earnest of a better place.

Grace, through Christ our Lord, is sent,
Leading sinners to repent;
Without money, without price,
To prepare us for the skies.

Grace, it is the peeping bud
Of the future wreath of God,
Promis'd in His holy word
To the servants of the Lord.

'Tis the penitent's first want,
But 'twill grow into a plant;
'Tis a longing to possess,
But that longing God will bless.

Grace, 'tis but the twilight ray
Of the Christian's glorious day,
But the foretaste of that store,
That will last for evermore.

VIII.

THERE is a sweet and welcome rest,
A day that God Himself hath blest,
An emblem of the land above,
Where all the saints do meet in love.

To-day our blessed Saviour rose,
And conquer'd all His mighty foes;
Come, let us sing His mighty deeds,
Who now for us poor sinners pleads.

There is a book I greatly prize;
No book so precious in mine eyes;

'Tis full of rich, eternal truth,
To cheer our age, and guide our youth.

Its promises are all divine;
O, may those promises be mine!
This, gracious Lord, is all my prayer,
The blessings of Thy saints to share.

There is a people that I love,
Who seek a country far above;
They are the exc'llent of the earth,
Superior to unholy mirth.

May I with them my cross still bear,
In all their sorrows take a share!
With them hereafter may I be,
Their blessed Lord and mine to see!

IX.

On Reading the "Memoir of the Author of 'The Sinner's Friend.'"

Is God thy Friend?—rejoice, O man,
That ever blessed truth to find!
Rejoice that ever love began
Within the great eternal Mind!

Is God thy Friend? infinite grace
That rear'd the structure of all good,
Extended to our fallen race!
Becoming our Redeemer, God.

Is God thy Friend, and cares for thee,
O sinful and rebellious man?
Let heaven and earth astonish'd be,
And wonder at God's saving plan!

Is Christ thy Friend? was He divest
Awhile of glory for thy sake,
And in our human nature dress'd,
That thou His glory might'st partake?

Is Christ thy Friend, made poor for thee,
And had not where to lay His head,
That thou might'st rich hereafter be,
Rich—with eternal manna fed?

Is Christ thy Friend? did he become
A sufferer in the vale of tears,
That thou, in heaven, might'st have a home,
And near Him spend eternal years?

Is Christ thy Friend? did He endure
The punishment of all thy guilt,
To make thy hope of heaven secure?
O, may His love thy spirit melt!

Is Christ thy Friend, and did He die
A cruel, agonizing death,
To make thy peace with God on high,
To save thee from eternal wrath?

Is Christ thy Friend, and does he plead
Thy cause before His Father's throne,
And there, to ratify the deed
Doth send the Holy Spirit down?

And is the Holy Ghost thy friend,
Still urging thee to seek the Lord?
To this blest Monitor attend!
His teachings comfort will afford.

And is the triune God thy friend,
Still calling, pressing thee to pray?
Do Father, Son, and Spirit blend
In One,—teaching the living way?

Then, sinner, canst thou still resist
Such great and such stupendous love?
From thy impenitence desist,
And seek those heights and depths to prove.

X.

WHEN waking, or when sleeping,
   O Lord, my Guardian be,
My spirit ever keeping
   In fellowship with Thee!

O, when I feel quite weary,
   And scarce can onward press,
Reveal Thy kindness clearly;—
   For Jesus' sake then bless.

Thou seest, each passing minute,
   The workings of my mind;
Thy goodness is infinite,
   Its depths I cannot find.

Struck with the deepest wonder
   At all Thy works and ways,

I tremble at Thy thunder,
And yet, adoring, praise!

I feel a solid pleasure
In contemplating Thee,
My Father, Saviour, Treasure,
O, still be near to me!

XI.

JUSTIFICATION AND SANCTIFICATION.

WHEN we believe in Christ, then we are justified:
When we believe that Jesus for our sins hath died,
That moment from all condemnation we are free,
And Jesus' righteousness imputed ours to be.

But still we have an evil heart of unbelief,
And oft we have to mourn, to sorrow, and to grieve
O'er our rebellious will, which we cannot subdue:
But God the Spirit comes, our spirits to renew.

When He begins His work, He comes so gently nigh,
Like as the morning light first breaking o'er the sky,
From grace and truth and light, to grace and truth
          and light,
He leads us onward still still, conquering in the fight.

At once through faith in Christ, we're freed from
          guilt of sin,
But a *progressive change*, the Spirit works within:
A holy, happy life, the blest result will be,
When, Spirit of the Lord, our souls are cleans'd by
          Thee.

XII.

"To be with Christ is Far Better."

Blest thought, to be where Jesus is,
To drink that pure and solid bliss
   That flows from His redeeming love ;
To be delivered from all sin,
From all impurities within,
   And dwell with holy saints above !

It is refreshing, and 'tis sweet,
Our blessed Jesus here to meet,
   In this imperfect, changing land ;
But greater far our bliss will be,
When our beloved Lord we see,
   And in His sacred presence stand !

When shall I join that happy throng,
And sing with them the new made song
   Of Jesus, and His matchless love ?
When shall I walk with Him in white,
Where faith and hope are lost in sight ?
   And His eternal goodness prove ?

V.

Prayer.

I.

CHRISTIAN, why your eye bedimm'd?
Why your heart with sorrow brimm'd?
Why escapes the frequent sigh?
Is not God your Helper nigh?

Do you mourn because of sin?
Mourn corruptions yet within?
Mourn your littleness of love?
Fear to grieve your God above?

Do you mourn a weakly faith
In His Providence who saith
" I will never thee forsake?"—
Mourning Christian comfort take.

If you have not, you may ask;
'Tis an easy, pleasant task.
Open to the Lord your heart,
And your troubles will depart.

Hasten to the throne of grace;
'Tis erected for our race,
Tell the Lord of every care;
O, be often pleading there!

Ours the duty 'tis to knock;
Thus God's treasures we unlock:
Ours the guilt if we neglect;
Thus God's treasures we reject.

II.

In earnest supplication,
In week or sabbath day,
In every age and station,
Lord, teach us how to pray!

When sin and fear perplex us,
And fill us with dismay,
When trials do distress us,
Lord, teach us then to pray!

To ask still without ceasing,
Though difficult the way,
Though comforts be decreasing,
Lord, give us grace to pray!

To seek, O heavenly Father,
Thy blessing on our way,
Though darkest clouds should gather,
Lord, help us still to pray!

To knock with faith unfailing,
While here on earth we stay;
In Jesus' name prevailing,
Lord, ever let us pray!

III.

JAMES V. 13.

Pray when all things seem bad,
Pray when you feel most sad:
O, listen to this exhortation!
Fulfil it to the letter,

And you will feel much better
Than spending time in lamentation.

Thank God if you are glad,
Lest you again be sad :
Give Him your hearty admiration :
In all your gladsome feelings,
Confess His gracious dealings,
'Tis He deserves your adoration.

VI.

Affliction.

I.

'Tis Thee, great God, 'tis Thee we love;
　How kind are all Thy ways!
Thy chastisements, how sweet they prove,
　When sanctified by grace!

How soft, how gently Thou dost smite
　Thy wandering children here!
Our earthly comforts Thou dost blight,
　To bring religion near.

When sad, perplex'd with many a care,
　And trouble clouds our brow,
Thou dost, O Lord, our hearts prepare,
　Far nobler joys to know.

When earth recedes, and comforts droop,
　And one by one depart,
Thou art an all sustaining Prop,
　To every trusting heart.

'Tis Thee, great God, 'tis Thee we trust,
　With calmness and repose,
Till light and glory on us burst,
　And all these evils close!

II.

AFFLICTION makes all things so dear,
　Belonging to the Lord,

The means of grace that we have here,
   His people, and His word.

Thus, far more precious unto me,
   The things of heaven than earth,
More precious far they prove to be
   In value and in worth.

Blest be the Lord, though on a couch
   Of weakness, and of pain,
This blessed truth I sure can vouch,
   Affliction is my gain.

Though from the busy world confin'd,
   From its engagements free,
I have engagements more refin'd,
   And suited unto me.

III.

THOUGH in deep affliction's gloom,
   Though of health and strength bereft,
Yet within, sweet joy hath room,
   For, my Saviour, Thou art left.

Though all earthly good decay,
   Which is short-liv'd good, at best,
Yet, my Saviour, if Thou stay,
   I shall be content and blest.

Though I feel dejected, sad,
   And with earthly things cast down,
Yet in Thee I will be glad,
   When all comforts else are gone.

Though I have no settled place,
No abiding city here,
I will triumph in Thy grace,
For, my Saviour, Thou art near.

Though my earthly frame decay,
Though my days are number'd here,
Though on earth I cannot stay,
I am free from care and fear.

Welcome death, disease, and all
Harbingers of coming rest:
Though I prematurely fall,
Yet my Saviour knows what's best.

Him I love, and Him I trust,
Ever blessed be His name !
I shall soon be with the just,
Fir'd with an immortal flame.

Then, how loud, how long I'll sing
When before my Saviour's face,
While the heav'nly cities ring
With the echoes of His grace!

IV.

CHILD of sickness and of grief,
Go to Jesus for relief,
He can comfort in distress,
In affliction he can bless.
Let but patience still abide,
Trust in Jesus crucified ;
This will all thy evils cure—
This will happiness ensure.

Child of sorrow and of woe,
Cease to trust in things below,
Cease to struggle with the wind :—
Look not back on things behind,
Look within with honest care,
See what wickedness is there ;
Then acknowledge the full truth,
To the God of age and youth.

Child of misery within,
Strive not to conceal thy sin ;
Haste to Jesus,--tell Him all,—
Of thy sins, and of thy fall.
Jesus knows thy state of need,
Jesus is a friend indeed ;
He will pity in distress :
Learn in pain His name to bless.

v.

Jesus, from thy blessed fulness,
    Let a sinner freely take ;
O, sustain me in each illness,
    Never, never me forsake !

While I tread this vale of mortals,
    Guide me with Thy gracious hand ;
Ere I come to death's dark portals,
    Fit me for that happier land.

Visit me with Thy salvation,
    Give to me a hope divine,
Make me one of that blest nation,
    Who as stars for ever shine !

VII.

Personal Recollections.

I.

God of my life, I bless thy name !
From Thee my early comforts came ;
   Thy wisdom chose my place ;
And gave me life in this blest land,
Where I can read and understand
   The message of Thy grace.

Thy Providence did fix my lot,
In yonder rural humble cot,
   Where first my life began.
To yonder Sabbath-school I went,
When hour on hour I happy spent,
   And time with pleasure ran.

Can I forget my native place ?
Can I forget those happy days ?
   Its scenes are fresh and clear.
Can I forget the friends I lov'd,
Whose Christian kindness there I prov'd ?
   To memory they are dear.

Author of talents, Thee I bless
For every good that I possess ;
   Great are Thy gifts to me.
Thou didst instruct me in my youth,
To seek the ever blessed truth
   Which is reveal'd by Thee.

And when I wander'd from Thy side,
And did not in Thy truth abide,
　　Still Thou didst o'er me watch.
When I rebell'd against Thy grace,
Forbearing mercy kept its place,
　　And did from ruin snatch.

How deep my guilt, how hard my heart,
When I did from the Lord depart.
　　And wander'd on in sin.
He might have left me to my ways,
But ever blessed be His grace,
　　That melted me within.

Strange were Thy ways to bring me back,
Of sufferings, Lord, I did not lack,
　　Deep misery I drank.
Full to the brim, and well nigh spent,
My passage rough, my comforts sent,
　　I found the world a blank.

When stripp'd of all, 'twas then I fled,
To seek a refuge in the shed
　　That God had plac'd for me.
With earnest prayer I onward ran,
Resolv'd no more to trust in man,
　　Nor aught on earth that be.

For ever blessed be the Hand
That shook the place where I did stand.
　　But sav'd my soul alive.
For what is earth, compar'd to souls?
'Tis as a speck on distant poles :
　　Far higher we must strive.

Hard were the sufferings I endur'd,
Before I could be well assur'd
  That sin was their first cause.
Hard were the struggles in my breast,
Before I found the solid rest
  Which now from Jesus flows.

Blest be the Eye that pitied me,
The Voice which call'd me back to see
  God's mercy and His love.
Blest be the Hand outstretch'd to save,
That kept me from an early grave,
  And fix'd my thoughts above.

Blessing, and praise, and glory be
To Him whose love hath conquered me,
  And savèd me from hell.
O Lord, increase my faith and love!
Let me for ever, ever prove,
  That Thou dost all things well.

O, may my heart and life be Thine!
Thy blessed will, Lord, make it mine!
  I would submit to Thee.
Stretch out Thy kind, protecting wings:
Save me from sin, O King of Kings,
  Till I Thy beauty see.

II.

WHEN standing on the verge of death,
And friends were whisp'ring round my bed,
And watching each succeeding breath,
And thinking soon I should be dead.

What blessed, happy moments those,
When I had bid farewell to all,
Waiting for death the scene to close,
Waiting my dear Redeemer's call.

For more than once or twice I've stood,
To all appearance on death's brink,
But power divine has stemm'd the flood,
And kept me that I did not sink.

And Jesus who did comfort me.
In view of my immediate death,
Will surely my Sustainer be,
Long as I draw this fleeting breath.

In view of life I tremble, Lord,
Lest I should sin against Thy love,
Do Thou sufficient grace afford,
And all perplexing fears remove.

Still keep me humble at Thy feet,
Give me a greater love to prayer:
And when my journey is complete
Receive me to Thy mansions fair.

III.

ON THE ANNIVERSARY OF HER ENTRANCE INTO THE WORKHOUSE.

WITH death full in view, I entered this place;
But God has been pleas'd to lengthen my days.
My path has been rugged, and thorny, and sad,
But the Lord, He has blest me, and made me feel glad.

I wish not to mention my trouble and grief;
I'll speak of my Saviour who oft sends relief.
I wish not to tell of my tossings and pain,
But of the great good which from Him I obtain.

His grace far exceeds my needs or my wants,
Provision for soul and for body He grants;
Accept of my heart, Lord, I yield it to Thee,
My Helper, and Friend, and Shepherd still be.

IV.

WHEN Jesus met me with His love,
In what a wretched state was I!
How sad and cheerless all did prove,
Before I found my Saviour nigh!

I dreamt I saw the judgment day!
Dread soon awoke me from my sleep;
It made me think upon my way,
And left impressions strong and deep!

Appall'd, and struck with deep amaze,
My heavy guilt I could not bear:
Then I began to sue for grace,
With earnest, persevering prayer.

And Jesus on my path did shine,
And thus he met me with His love,
And gave me happiness divine,
And precious unto me did prove.

v.

SABBATH SCHOOL REMINISCENCES.

THE Sabbath School forgetting!
O, this can never be!
In days of nervous fretting,
I ponder still o'er thee.

I lov'd my Sabbath teachers,
Yes, every one of them ;
And still to memory reaches
Each visage and each name.

But some have cross'd the river,
And enter'd on their rest,
To praise the Lord for ever,
Who made their labour blest.

And some are yet remaining,
Still toiling here below ;
But time is on them gaining,
And wrinkling fast their brow.

O, may the Lord of heaven,
Grant us to meet above,
Where joys are ever given,
And all are fill'd with love !

VIII.
Expressive of the Author's own Feelings.

I.

Lord, I will trust Thee every day,
　　May faith from Thee be given !
Take not my little faith away,
　　But send me more from heaven.

What shall I do while troubles last,
　　If not on thee depend ?
What shall I do when life is past,
　　If Thou art not my friend ?

What shall I do,—a guilty wretch,
　　Without forgiving love ?
Thine arm of mercy, Lord, outstretch ;
　　May I Thy goodness prove !

What shall I do when rocks shall rend,
　　And graves shall open'd be,
When all the righteous shall ascend,
　　If Thou shalt frown on me ?

O, what a thing to contemplate,
　　To prove a cast-away !
Lord Jesus, ere it be too late,
　　Prepare me for that day !

II.

Jesus, Thy name is ever dear,
And ever welcome unto me :
　c

Happy I feel when thou art near,
Though in the Workhouse still I be.

My lot on earth is poor and mean,
My circumstances sad indeed ;
But Jesus cheers the dreary scene :
He meets me in my greatest need.

He smiles on me, though some may frown,
He pities failings none can see ;
He welcomes me, whoe'er may spurn :
How kind my Jesus is to me !

He comforts and he succours me ;
He teaches me to look above,
Beyond this life and its rough sea,
To yonder land of rest and love.

He hushes all my passions still,
He makes the storm become a calm,
Brings sweet submission to his will,
And holds me with His mighty arm.

He makes the curse a blessing prove,
He turns my sorrow into joy,
He teaches this hard heart to love,
And make His praises my employ.

He turns my darkness into light,
He makes this earth become a heaven,
Gives inward peace 'midst outward fright :
All glory to his name be given !

III.

BELOVED Saviour, without Thee,
Where could my trembling spirit rest?
What could I do, or whither flee?
Of Thy salvation unpossess'd?
But, ever blessed be Thy name,
Thy love exceeds my guilt and shame.

I dare not look upon my guilt,
Only through Thy forgiving love :
I know Thy precious blood was spilt,
My condemnation to remove ;
This calms my fears, this soothes my mind,
And joy and peace in thee I find.

I dare not look Death in the face,
Nor ponder on the gloomy grave,
But through the medium of Thy grace,
And the assurance Thou canst save :
Thy promises are firm and sure,
And hence my hope is made secure.

IV.

Jesus, I own Thy gracious sway,
As coming from above ;
Through grace I tread the narrow way,
I fear, I trust, I love.

I fear Thee with a filial fear,
Apart from slavish dread ;
I wish to glorify Thee here,
My Saviour, Husband, Head.

I trust Thee for all things to come ;
　I seek no will but Thine ;
Give me, amidst all earthly gloom,
　Submission, deep, divine.

I love Thee for Thy dying love,
　For Thou didst die for me ;
Give me a mansion far above,
　That I may dwell with Thee.

V.

JESUS, Thy love I fain would sing,
　In soft and touching lays ;
And round Thy name I fain would fling
　Attraction's lovely rays.

Jesus, Thy truths I fain would spread,
　With an untiring zeal,
That many others may be led
　Those blessed truths to feel.

Jesus, in earnest prayer I write
　My plain unletter'd lines ;
O, may Thy Spirit words indite
　From wisdom's sacred mines !

Jesus, my Spirit truly burns,
　While I pursue my task ;
Mine eye of faith to Thee still turns,
　And doth Thy guidance ask.

Jesus, it does me good to speak
　Of Thee, and of Thy name ;

And pleasant labour 'tis to seek
That all may feel the same.

VI.

If I can nearer come to Thee,
And drink still deeper of Thy love,
And more and more devoted be,
    And faithful prove ;—

If, through Thy Holy Spirit, I
Can lead one sinner unto Thee,
To seek for better joys on high,
    And holy be ;—

If through the influence of Thy grace,
I can do but the smallest good,
Then lengthen out my mortal days,
    O blessed God !

If I can glorify Thy name,
And honour Thee, my dearest Lord,
I'll covet neither wealth nor fame,
    But trust Thy word.

But, Lord, I covet stronger faith,
And brighter hopes, and deeper love :
O, sanctify me until death !
    My Keeper prove.

And if it be Thy blessed will,
Renew my health, restore my strength ;
To my diseases say, " Be still,
    You've reach'd your length."

If not,—I know Thy ways are just,
And holy, wise, and righteous still,
In either case, Lord, I will trust
       Thy blessed will.

VII.

O, BOUND, my heart, for joy!
Jesus did come to save.
Praise be my sweet employ;
Himself for me He gave.
Can I ask more, can I need less
Than Jesus' death and righteousness?

No name to me so dear,
No subject half so sweet;
I feel Thy presence near,
I worship at Thy feet.
Still give me grace to trust in Thee,
Whate'er my situation be.

I feel my weakness, Lord,
I tremble, yet rejoice;
I listen to Thy word,
I hear the still, small voice.
Thou wilt not leave me to myself,
Nor sin, nor to its yawning gulph.

I give my all to Thee,
Thou precious, bleeding Lamb!
Thou wilt accept of me,
Unworthy though I am.
And had I more, it should be Thine;
I'd spend it in Thy cause divine.

VIII.

COMFORT FROM THE MUSE.

EXCEPT for this employment,
    The muse's pleasant care,
Small would be my enjoyment,
    Throughout the passing year.

Confin'd within the Union,
    Feeble and listless both,
Sweet muse, in thy communion,
    My days are chiefly smooth.

I feel I've many failings,
    Which I cannot explain ;
But I have had rough sailings,*
    Which did my spirits drain.

I feel such great exhaustion,
    Full many times a day,
And such a strange sensation,
    As if to pass away.

I do not feel surprisèd
    At my condition now,
For I have realisèd
    Much trouble, want, and woe.

Nought but God's care infinite
    In dangers kept me safe,
Watch'd over me each minute,
    Preserving from the grave.

*A conventional expression.

Then on His care relying,
    May I be ever found :
To Him in trouble flying
    Whose goodness knows no bound !

IX.

THOUGH distress doth still abound,
Though afresh on me it breaks,
I would be submissive found,
To the Lord who gives and takes.

Startling is the news I hear,
(How it harrows up my heart !)
Of an only brother dear,
Call'd with sight and health to part.

Never able more to earn,
For his children, daily bread :
From the prospect, O, I turn ;
It bewilders my poor head.

Sight is a most precious thing,
Precious 'tis as ought we have :
When it waves a farewell wing,
Life is cheerless, sad, and grave.

Health, it is a boon indeed,
When it is enjoyed in full,
While we earn our daily bread,
And the sweets of labour cull.

If I have a wish to live,
'Tis that I may labour still,
And to my dear children give
Daily bread, and clothes at will.

I have labour'd in past time,
But the scene is changèd now :
When the clock for six does chime,
To my work I cannot go.

Strength is gone, and health is fled :
To this low condition brought,
Lord, sustain my drooping head,
And remove each murm'ring thought !

X.
AFTER A SEASON OF TEMPTATION.

l.

DARK the path I lately trod ;
Satan nearly did destroy
All my confidence in God :
Fearfully he did annoy.

Hard the conflict, and as strange,
The suggestions he did use ;
But the Lord the scene did change
And my harass'd spirit loose.

Though the Lord may seem to frown,
And sometimes to hide His face,
If we really are His own,
He will visit us with grace.

Naught can ever separate
His own people from His love.
Though the wicked world may hate,
All will for the better prove.

XI.

AFTER A SEASON OF TEMPTATION.

2.

THE sigh is gone, the tear is spent,
   The struggle all is o'er,
Now I can give my joy full vent,
   And my blest Lord adore.

'Tis true, the struggle has been hard,
   Painful to flesh and sense;
But now, I more and more regard
   God's gracious Providence.

My children, Lord, I now can leave
   To Thy unerring care;
And, by Thy help, I will not grieve,
   Nor yield to sad despair.

When in the grave I low am laid,
   Upon my children look;
And O, may their poor names be found
   Writ in the Saviour's Book!

XII.

COMPOSED IN PROSPECT OF DEATH.

My stay on earth long will not be,
   My strength is failing fast,
And soon it will be said of me,
   Her mortal life is past.

But God be prais'd, this truth I know,
   That He is ever kind,
All who seek Him in their woe
   Are sure His grace to find.

Affliction, sorrow, pain, and death,
   Are messengers of love ;
He sends them here to try our faith,
   And draw our hearts above.

XIII.*

I would be humbl'd 'neath His hand,
Who has my whole at His command.
Though He has wounded, He will heal,
And I again shall comfort feel.

I would submit to all His will,
Who orders both my good and ill,
Trusting He knoweth what is best :
And unto Him I'd leave the rest.

I would love God with love intense,
For He loves me with love immense ;
Would trust His mighty, saving arm,
In times of fear or peaceful calm.

I would have Jesus ever near,
For His blest presence rids my fear.
O, may He guide me safely home,
To share the promis'd good to come !

* Composed the latest in the collection.

IX.

To the Chairman of the Board of Guardians.

Excuse me for addressing
These humble lines to you,
My grateful thanks expressing,
To all the Guardians due.

In widow'd destitution,
I to this place did flee ;
But for such Institution,
What would become of me ?

What could I do in sickness ?
I could not earn my bread,
Nor in my present weakness,
Unto the factory tread.

Oft with myself communing,
I think what ills would come,
Unless within this Union,
My children had a home.

Here females are protected
From insult and from shame ;
The rules, so well directed,
Bring credit to your name.

How honour'd your position,
  In reference to this place,
Fulfilling your commission,
  With all becoming grace.

Long may your health be glowing,
  Long be your labours here,
In estimation growing
  Higher each passing year.

In that esteem a sharer
  Be every Guardian too,
And every office-bearer,
  As unto each is due.

X.

On the Deaths of the Inmates of the Workhouse.

I.

RACHEL DAWSON,

An aged woman, of Christian character, who had lived in the
House about five years, and died in the adjoining bed
to that of GRACE DICKINSON.

Poor RACHEL is gone—what a happy release
From sickness and sorrow, from pain, and from death!
Poor RACHEL is gone—her end, O, 'twas peace!
How sweetly she died, supported by faith!

Poor RACHEL is gone—how sweetly she went!
Encircled with arms of infinite love.
Poor RACHEL is gone—for Jesus hath sent,
And call'd her to dwell in mansions above.

Poor RACHEL is gone—how welcome the rest!
How glorious, and happy, and blessed the change!
May such be our lot, to meet with the blest,
Unblemish'd with sin in glory to range!

O, may we adore redemption's blest scheme,
On earth and in heaven for ever, O Lord!
And ever rejoice in the wonderful theme
Made known unto us in Thy written word. ·

II.

ELLEN HAIGH,

A woman about 60 years of age, who died a few weeks after being brought to the House.

ANOTHER visit Death has paid,
Another sister low is laid ;
But she had hope, for she did pray,
And Jesus turns not one away.

Oft in the stillness of the night,
I heard her pray for strength and light ;
For strength to bear as well as do,
For light to guide her safely through.

What though her sufferings were severe ?
Her Saviour's love her heart did cheer ;
And she did, with a sweet delight,
All her concerns to Him commit.

Oft have I heard her bless His name :
And if on earth,—in heaven the same
Shall be the utterance of her soul—
" Glory to God who's all in all. "

Ye sick, prepare your God to meet,
By sitting at your Saviour's feet :
O, learn of Him who loves to save,
Whose blessings reach beyond the grave !

III.

ELIZABETH BARKER.

JESUS, we recognize Thy grace,
We recognize Thy gracious hand ;
Thy wisdom and Thy goodness trace,
Though Death has visited our band,
    And taken hence
Boor BETTY to another land.

We sorrow, and we feel her loss,
Yet not without a Christian hope:
We feel her absence, miss her voice,
And yet the gospel bears us up ;
    This light doth shine
When every other light doth droop.

We trust that she is now on high,
Exulting in that blessed land,
Where not a sorrow, nor a sigh,
Shall ever mar that happy band.
    Lord grant that we
May meet and dwell at Thy right hand !

XI.

𝔉or the 𝔜oung.

I.

PRAYER FOR A CHILD.*

BLESSED Lord, I come to Thee,
Though a little child I be :
Thou dost see me every day,
When I work and when I play.

Help me, Lord, to feel aright,
When I say my prayers to-night.
I would not a trifler be,
For I know Thou seest me.

'Tis in Jesus' name I come.
Lord, I thank Thee for my home,
For my health, and for my bread,
For my raiment, and my bed,

For my father, mother dear,
For my brothers, sisters near;
To Thy care I these commend ;
Heavenly Father, be their Friend.

Bless them for their care of me :
Help me to obedient be ;
Help me, Lord, to speak the truth,
In my childhood, and my youth.

Help me not to steal nor cheat,
Nor bad language to repeat ;

* Inserted in No. 442 of the "Sunday at Home."

Help me in Thy fear to live,
And to all due honour give.

Help me, Lord, help me, I pray,
To love Jesus every day ;
May my sins be all forgiven :
Take me when I die to heaven.

II.

Lord, help us, when we worship Thee,
    To worship Thee in truth :
May we sincere and earnest be.
    Forgive our trifling youth.

Lord, help us, when we sing Thy praise,
    To praise Thee with our heart ;
And not to mock Thee in our lays,
    For that's a wicked part.

Lord, help us, when we hear Thy word,
    To hear with solemn awe :
Thy Spirit unto us afford,
    That we may profit draw.

Lord, help us, while on earth we stay,
    To yield ourselves to Thee,
To travel in the narrow way,
    And thus true Christians be.

Lord, help us, in our latest breath,
    To put our trust in Thee ;
Sustain us in the hour of death,
    And our Salvation be.

XII.

Miscellaneous.

I.

THE NEW YEAR.

1.

A NEW year,—'tis a pleasant time,
Recalling recollections dear,
Sweetly to memory it doth chime,
As if it brought past seasons near.

A new year,—'tis a pleasant sound,
Telling of mercies and of joys ;
How fast the seasons do pass round,
Making creation to rejoice.

A new year,—then the old one's past,
With all its sorrows and its tears ;
But its remembrance long shall last,
Far, far beyond these rolling years.

A new year,—'tis in mercy sent
A mercy added to the rest.
Lord, in Thy fear may it be spent,
And with Thy blessing be it blest !

2.

ANOTHER fleeting year its course has run,
Another period has its course begun,
    And, "onward, onward," is Time's motto still.

How rapidly we travel to the tomb!
Approaching near and nearer to death's gloom,
  As on we tread each vale and rugged hill.

Many within the year just past have died,
And many others have their place supplied,
  But we are spar'd, and still on earth we live.
And yet, we know not what a day may bring!
Disease and death are ever on the wing,
  And soon our last account we too must give.

O Lord, we pray Thee, send Thy Spirit down!
Our life, our time, and all our mercies crown,
  With the sweet drawings of Thy grace and love.
For death and judgment, Lord, our souls prepare,
And grant that we may life eternal share,
  When from this earth Thou call'st us to remove.

THE BUSINESS OF LIFE.

Our time is short, our work is great,
  'Tis much we have to do;
Eternal soon will be our state,
  Eternity's in view.

To flee from sin, from sin to part,
  Sin evermore disown;
To worship God with all our heart,
  To worship Him alone;—

To value not the world, nor fall,
  Nor linger, at its shrine;
To bear our cross, and give up all
  Oppos'd to grace divine;—

To wage a war with every lust,
  With every wicked thought;
To love what's holy, good, and just,
  With sweet obedience taught;—

To trust in Jesus Christ the Lord,
  To trust Him to the last;
To take Him ever at His word,
  Our all on Him to cast;—

To glorify our Father's name,
  And ever seek His will;
To love His saints with love's pure flame,
  To pray for sinners still;—

Thus to prepare for heaven above,
  'Tis a great work indeed!
But grace divine our souls can move,
  And thus to heaven can lead.

DEATH.

1.

AND is it thus appointed,
  That we must surely die?
Is life to be accounted
  A dream that passeth by?

And are all things thus tending?
  Do all to this point draw?
Yes,—all things seem befriending
  Death's universal law.

Diseases but precede him,
    Preparing for his stroke;
And war and famine speed him
    To hasten with his yoke.

Vain are the blooming roses,
    Upon the youthful face;
No age, nor state opposes
    Death's universal race.

And they who live the longest,
    But have a short respite;
And they who feel the strongest,
    With them 'twill soon be night.

Why is it thus ordainèd
    That every one must die?
In God's book is explainèd
    The very reason why.

It shows that through transgression,*
    Death to the world has come;
And hence 'tis our possession,
    Our heritage, our doom.

It points us to the Saviour
    Who His own life laid down,
To bring us to God's favour
    And save us from His frown;—

Who shrunk not from death's portal
    But pass'd into the grave,

* The last three verses have been altered by the Editor.

That, with His life immortal,
   He ruin'd man might save.

2.

DEATH truly is a solemn thing,
   But to the Christian's heart,
Much consolation it doth bring ;
   He longeth to depart.

It is his moment of release
   From all that can annoy ;
His entrance to the land of peace,
   His Saviour to enjoy.

May such a blessed lot be mine,
   When my short life is o'er,
Redeemer, Advocate divine,
   And I will ask no more !

CAUSES FOR WEEPING.

WELL may I weep, O God of love,
   When I look back and see
That I in wickedness did rove,
   That I've forsaken Thee !

Well may I weep, when I behold
   Thy cross my dying Lord ;
What depths of love it doth unfold,
   What tears of joy afford ?

Well may I weep, when men depart
   From Thee, the living way ;

For Thy dear cause lies near my heart,
And for its good I pray.

Well may I weep when men do slight
The offers of Thy grace,
Preferring darkness unto light,
Preferring strife to peace.

Well may I weep that men still wound
Jesus the sinner's Friend ;
Rejecting love without a bound,
And bliss without an end !

But O, there is a land divine,
Where I shall weep no more ;
Where grief shall not with joy entwine,
For 'tis a sinless shore !

AGAINST PROCRASTINATION.

WHY on the morrow's dawn presume ?
No promise that we see
Gives such presumption any room ;
Then foolish it must be.

Why yield to sin ? 'tis not the way
To gain the long'd for good :
Why not begin this very day,
To live for heaven and God ?

Why clutch the world with eager hand,
Why grasp it firmer still ?
The world is not at our command,
To gratify our will.

Ah ! why love sin, and tread its way ?
　'Tis a tormenting thing:
Permit it but to have its way,
　And ruin it will bring.

Then linger not upon the brink
　Of sin's most fatal stream,
But haste to Jesus, lest thou sink,
　And perish far from Him !

The Goodness of God.

There's not a living thing on earth,
　Nor in the mighty sea,
Great Author of Creation's birth,
　But it is fed by Thee.

There's not an insect in the air,
　How tiny it may be,
But has Thy kind and gracious care :
　All, all are kept by Thee.

And man though wicked, haughty, proud,
　Though he rebellious be,
Though in his language he is bold,
　He lives sustained by Thee.

Lord, help us, lead us to repent,
　Through Thy forbearance shown ;
Let not our earthly days be spent,
　To grieve and grieve Thee on.

O, give us grace to live to Thee,
　While life and time are given ;
Teach us to understand and see
　The purposes of heaven !

Against Repining.

THE present mercies we enjoy,
  How little they appear !
While mercies past our thoughts employ,
  And draw the trembling tear.

We think and talk upon past ills,
  Thus spoiling present good :
Then in our breast what anger fills,
  And heats our very blood.

Lord for the future give us grace,
  This sinfulness to shun ;
And in our thoughts, and words, and ways,
  Thy blessed will be done !

The Times of Persecution.

OFT muse I on the martyr's doom,
Imprison'd in a dungeon's gloom,
Fetter'd and bound with heavy chains,
None daring to assuage their pains.

Fines and imprisonments abound,
Where persecution rages round ;
The loss of all that they possess,
Who dare their Saviour to confess.

What trying circumstances theirs !
What tempting bribes, what deep-laid snares !
What wickedness the wicked find,
To teaze the true believer's mind !

Led forth amidst the multitude,
Assail'd by scoffs and insults rude,
To suffer death, because they love
The truth reveal'd from God above.

O, could I die for Jesus' sake ?
Could I endure the martyr's stake?
O, could I bear this trying test?
And, still unmov'd, on Jesus rest?

O, could I seal the truth with blood,
And thus bring glory to my God?
Still praising Him in every breath,
Rejoicing in the pangs of death?

These thoughts oft flash across my mind,
When in past history I find
The sad details of papal crimes,
And laws of persecuting times.

Blest be the Lord, that in this age,
These persecutions do not rage :
Blest be the Lord, for ever blest,
Who gives His churches peace and rest.

To the Twin Children of Mr. & Mrs. Tyerman,

on their First Birthday.

Lovely babes, but just expanding
To the light of opening day,
Our deep sympathies commanding,
As you wend your infant way.

You we love and yet we ponder
On the ills that you may meet ;
And we gaze on you the fonder,
As those ills we contemplate.

Born into a world of dangers,
Troubles, sorrows, fears, and sin;
Yet we hail you little strangers,
With a heart-felt joy within.

For 'twas God that you created,
And His work is never vain ;
Your existence he hath mated,
With the curious tie of twain.

May that God watch o'er your spirits,
As you tread the vale below ;
Through the blessed Saviour's merits
Bless, and guide, and help you through.

And ye parents, guardians, teachers,
Dedicate them to the Lord ;
In your hearts be living preachers,
Train them up to love His Word.

To a Bereaved Mother in America.

Excuse a far off stranger,
Who never saw your face,
Though I become a ranger,
In rhyme to reach your place.

And when these lines shall meet you,
  My boldness be forgiven :—
In Jesus' name I greet you ;
  Peace from the God of heaven !

To you I am addressing
  These lines in christian love ;
And may the Saviour's blessing
  Rest on them from above.

The trials of a mother
  The Lord alone doth know,
As one and then another
  Of her lov'd ones lies low.

And frames like ours, so tender,
  Such blows do greatly feel ;
But, God being our defender,
  All surely must be well.

The Lord is full of pity,
  And gently He doth lead
From sin's destructive city,
  His lov'd and chosen seed.

Then, in the Lord confiding,
  We cannot go astray ;
If in the truth abiding,
  'Twill smooth our rugged way.

O, may we meet in glory,
  And in immortal light,
To sing the joyful story,
  Our God doth all things right !

BLINDNESS.

An elderly woman afflicted with blindness, whom the Chaplain taught to read by the raised characters, requested G. D. to compose some verses, furnishing her with a few thoughts as an indication of what she wished.

SOMETIMES there is a sadness,
　　Which o'er my frame doth steal;
My darkness chills my gladness,
　　When I upon it dwell.

I muse on former seasons,
　　When I enjoy'd my sight;
And yet I've many reasons
　　To think my darkness right.

Why should I be repining,
　　With comforts near at hand?
Let me, O Lord, be trying
　　Thy will to understand.

'Tis God my sight hath smitten,
　　And what He does is right:
His promises are written
　　To be my better light.

It is my heavenly Father,
　　Then I will meekly bend,
Choose here to suffer, rather
　　Than perish in the end.

I muse then on my blindness,
　　In solemn, serious thought;

It teaches me God's kindness
   Which long I set at naught.

God's mercy brought me hither,
   Beneath His servant's care,
Though earthly prospects wither,
   My heavenly hopes are fair.

  *   *   *   *
    *   *   * †
He taught my soul most clearly
   To trust in Jesus' blood.

He taught me, with my fingers
   To read Thy blessed word,
*   *   *   *
    *   *   * †

Great God, forgive my folly
   In days for ever past :
Now make me pure and holy,
   Ere Death his shadows cast.

O Lord, illumine my spirit ‡
   With wisdom from above :
Let me Thy grace inherit,
   Yea, Thine eternal love !

† These lines are omitted as being of too personal a
   character for publication.

‡ Altered by the Editor.

To a Christian Friend.

WELCOME, although faint my smile,
Doubly welcome all the while ;
But when sickness seizeth me,
It doth make me gloomy be.

Thanks to God, for He is good,
Gives us all through Jesus' blood,
All we really need below,
Also grace to help us through.

Let us wait our Father's time,
Yield unto His will sublime,
Both in little things and great ;
Willing He should choose our state.

Thus, O Lord, to Thee we look,
Through each promise in Thy book ;
Thus will we for ever trust
Thee, the Father of the just.

Good Night.

GOOD night, dear friends, in Jesus' name,
May His blest Spirit fill your breast,
May He protect each tender frame,
And give you sweet refreshing rest.

And if you see to-morrow's dawn,
O may that dawn to Him be given !
In grateful praise approach His throne,
Let grateful praise ascend to heaven.

ALFRED W. STANFIELD, PRINTER, WAKEFIELD.